For my sister, Katherine, who encouraged me and was, perhaps, the bubble's biggest fan.
Also, to my husband, Michael, who I met right outside of Tiger Stadium, and for my precious children:
Tripp, Charlotte, and Joseph.

www.mascotbooks.com

THE BUBBLE'S DAY AT LSU

For more information, please contact:
Mascot Books
620 Herndon Parkway #320
Herndon, VA 20170
info@mascotbooks.com

CPSIA Code: PRT0721A
ISBN-13: 978-1-64543-924-0

Printed in the United States

THE BUBBLE'S DAY AT LSU

LSU

Written and Illustrated by
Rachel Chustz

One Saturday a bubble was blown.
The girl who did it couldn't have known
That this little bubble that she blew
Would spend the whole day at LSU.

As the little bubble rolled in the breeze,
She was briskly whisked through old oak trees.
She giggled as the leaves tickled her skin.
She knew an adventure would soon begin.

The bubble reached campus just in time
To hear the Memorial Tower chime.
Children looked with curiosity.
How could this magical bubble be?
They chased her across the Parade Grounds
Then followed her up and down the Indian Mounds.

The bubble heard a lively crowd
Shouting "Go Tigers!" loud and proud.
Tailgaters were set up everywhere,
And Tiger spirit filled the air.

Family and friends from out of town
Were talking and laughing all around.
They got quiet and gathered to see
This real-life bubble, a mystery.

The bubble just coasted right along
As she hummed the tune of "The Fight Song."
At Victory Hill, she made her descent,
Then right past Mike the Tiger she went.

The bubble tried her best to be discreet
But wound up in the middle of the street.
The football team saw her, the coaches did too.
They all stared in amazement as they marched through.

A little while later people swarmed
Up to the stadium and lines were formed.
In the gust of their wind the bubble went too.
When she got to the entrance, she zipped right through.

People watched as the bubble flew past.
The stadium was already filling up fast.
There were fans in purple, fans in gold,
Fans who were young, and fans who were old.
They ate Tiger Dogs and nachos too.
Cheerleaders shouted for LSU

When the mascot, Mike the Tiger, appeared
All of Death Valley applauded and cheered.
There was chatting and chanting everywhere
And pompoms were waving in the air.

It didn't take long for The Tigers to score,
And the crowd let out a magnificent roar.
Touchdown for The Tigers again and again
And soon the half-time show would begin.

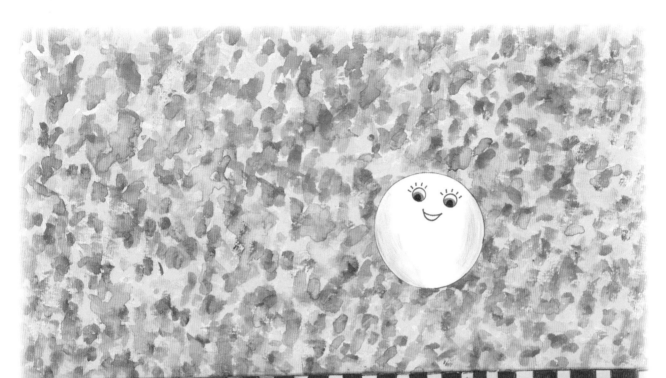

A wave began to circle the stands
As people stood and lifted their hands.
As their arms moved faster, the bubble went round.
She surfed the whole crowd, then was blown to the ground.

Next was the talented Golden Band
Straight from the famous Tigerland.
They played shiny instruments and marched in lines.
They crisscrossed and wove into fancy designs.

THE GOLDEN BAND FROM TIGERLAND

The bubble enjoyed her front row seat.
Her body shook to the drummer's beat.
The conductor's arms fluttered and flapped.
The bubble fretted as cymbals clapped.

She floated right down to the fifty-yard line.
Spectators were scared, but the bubble was fine.
The bubble then danced with the Golden Girls,
Bouncing in the wind of their kicks and twirls.
The bubble laughed as she flipped up and down.
The Golden Girls smiled as they all spun around.

Tiger Stadium went wild when they finished the show.
The bubble was the star, and she didn't even know.
Everyone in the stands was quite amazed
That the bubble was completely unfazed.

As the trumpet let out its final blast,
It shot the bubble through the air so fast.
The crowd gasped as she flew to the sky.
She went up and up, higher than high.

Finally, the bubble was among the stars.
The stadium twinkled so bright from afar.
The bubble watched so excitedly
As The Tigers claimed their victory.

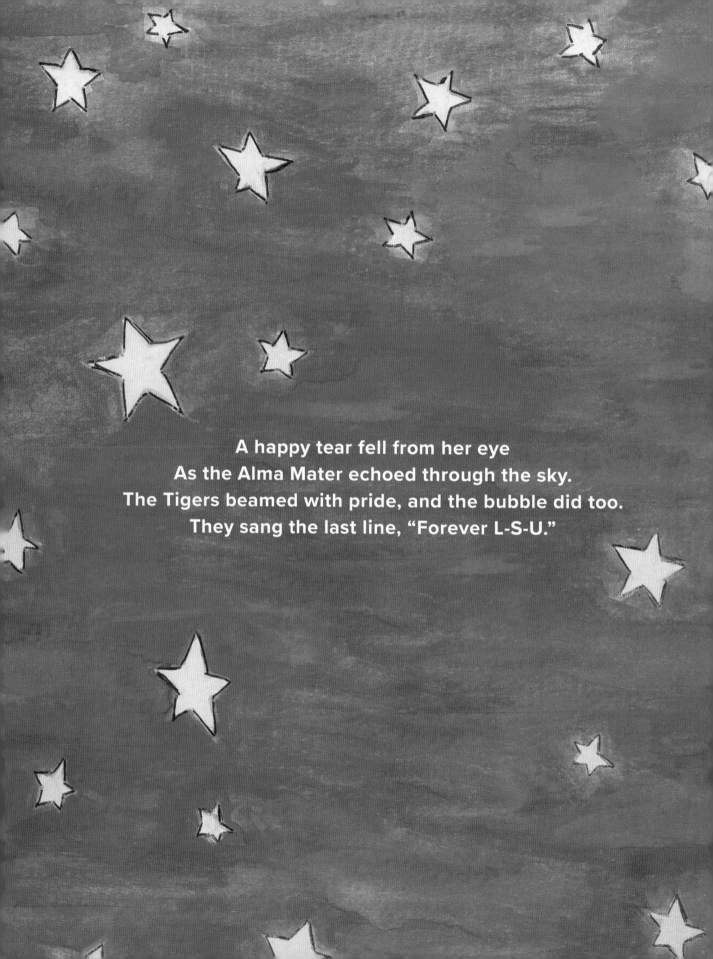

A happy tear fell from her eye
As the Alma Mater echoed through the sky.
The Tigers beamed with pride, and the bubble did too.
They sang the last line, "Forever L-S-U."